DOG PARK

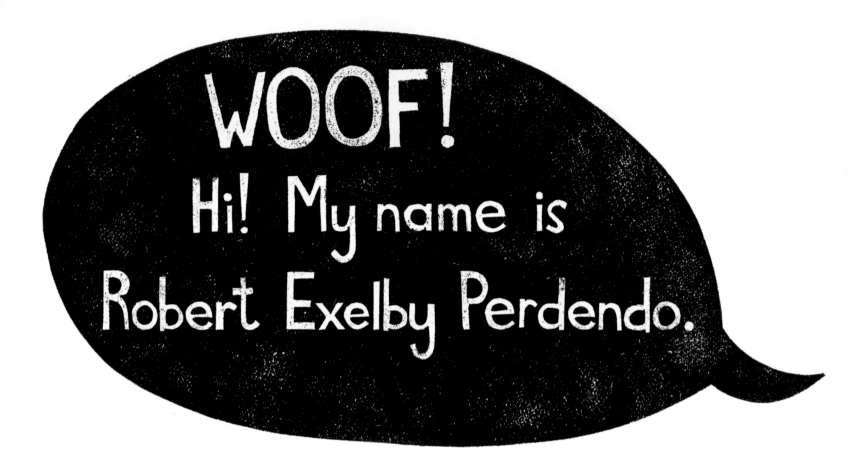

But everyone calls me Lazybones
because I don't like going out.

This is Dad.

We have a lot of fun together.

I really like teaching him new tricks.
He's a very fast learner!

And I've trained him to give me treats!

But there's one little problem.
I just want to stay at HOME.

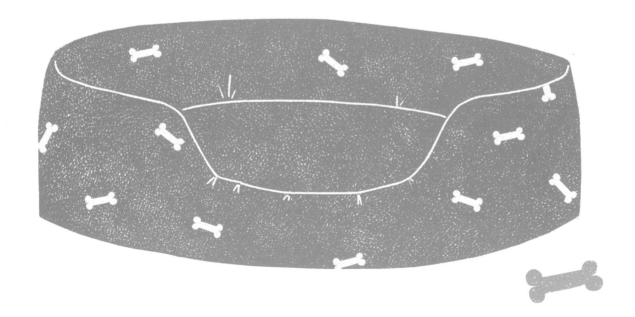

So when I hear him shout...

I run and hide.

I'm getting pretty good at it.
See?

Some hiding places are very smelly.

Where are you, you Lazybones?

And some are very wet,
but I don't mind.

I don't always have time to hide.
So then I pretend I'm sleeping.

But if he finds me...

Then I *have* to go out on walkies.

So I try to get home again as fast as I can.

It's the WORST when he stops to gossip.
Nobody ever talks to *me*.

But last week something
different happened.

And I knew just what game to play.
Hide-and-seek!

I did my best-ever hide.
Pretty soon, everyone was playing.
And they were all searching for ME!

I'll just have a look around.

Wow!
He's really good.

They looked and looked.
Can you see me?

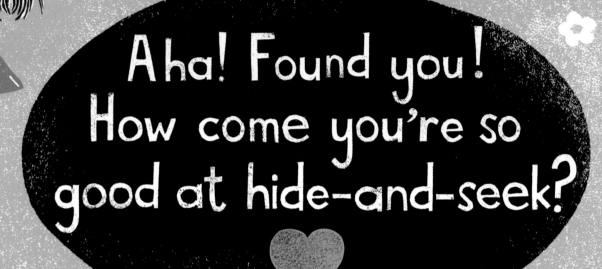

Oh, I've played it at home once or twice.
But it's even more fun with all of you!

Now I love going out ALL the time!

Now who's the lazybones?